TITCH

by PAT HUTCHINS

Aladdin Paperbacks

Aladdin Paperbacks
An imprint of Simon & Schuster
Children's Publishing Division
1230 Avenue of the Americas
New York, NY 10020
First Aladdin Paperbacks edition, 1993
Printed in the United States of America
20 19 18 17 16 15 14 13 12 11

Library of Congress Cataloging-in-Publication Data
Hutchins Pat. 1942-
    Titch / by Pat Hutchins
        p.   cm.
    Summary: Titch feels left out because he is so much smaller than his
brother and sister until he gets a little seed that grows bigger than anything
they have.
    ISBN 0-689-71688-5
    [1. Size—Fiction.   2. Brothers and sisters—Fiction.]   I. Title.
    PZ7H96165Ti   1993
[E]—dc20   92-1642

For Darren

Titch was little.

His sister Mary
was a bit bigger.

And his brother Pete
was a lot bigger.

Pete had a great big bike.

Mary had a big bike.

And Titch had a little tricycle.

Pete had a kite
that flew high
above the trees.

Mary had a kite
that flew high
above the houses.

And Titch had a pinwheel
that he held in his hand.

Pete had a big drum.

Mary had a trumpet.

And Titch had
a little wooden whistle.

Pete had a big saw.

Mary had a big hammer.

And Titch held the nails.

Pete had a big spade.

Mary had a fat flowerpot.

But Titch had the tiny seed.

And Titch's seed grew

and grew

and grew.